D1584098

).uk   **To order:**
more information about   ☎ Phone 0845 6044371
Raintree books.   🖹 Fax +44 (0) 1865 312263
                           🖳 Email myorders@capstonepub.co.uk

Customers from outside the UK please telephone +44 1865 312262

Raintree is an imprint of Capstone Global Library Limited, a company
incorporated in England and Wales having its registered office at 7 Pilgrim
Street, London, EC4V 6LB – Registered company number: 6695582

"Raintree" is a registered trademark of Pearson Education Limited,
under licence to Capstone Global Library Limited

Text © Stone Arch Books, 2008
First published in United Kingdom by Capstone Global Library in 2010
The moral rights of the proprietor have been asserted.

Edited in the UK by Laura Knowles
Art Director: Heather Kindseth
Graphic Designer: Kay Fraser
Originated by Captone Global Library Ltd
Printed and bound in China by CTPS

Photo Credits
Karon Dubke, cover

ISBN 978 1 40621 582 3 (hardback)
14 13 12 11 10
10 9 8 7 6 5 4 3 2 1

ISBN 978 1 406215 97 7 (paperback)
14 13 12 11 10
10 9 8 7 6 5 4 3 2 1

British Library Cataloguing in Publication Data
Brezenoff, Steven.
Alley of shadows. -- (School mysteries)
813.6-dc22
A full catalogue record for this book is available from the British Library.

CONTENTS

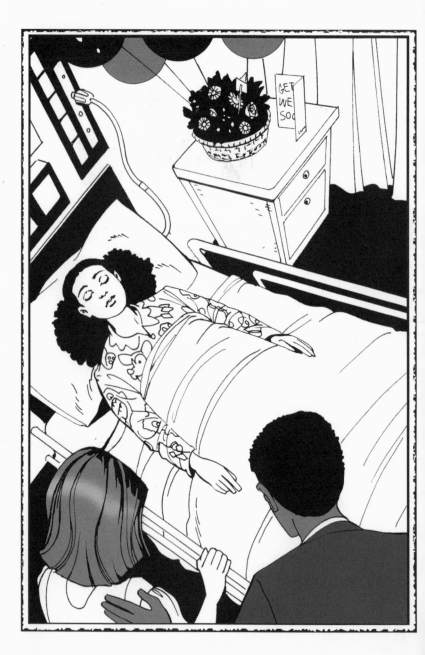

THE GIRL IN ROOM 424

A thirteen-year-old girl lay unconscious in room 424 of River City General Hospital.

She had been in a coma since the ambulance workers brought her in several nights earlier.

There was always at least one visitor at her bedside.

Tonight was no different.

Tonight, her parents stood nearby and gazed down at their daughter.

She was wearing pink cartoon pyjamas and her eye was badly bruised.

The girl did not know they were there.

The girl did not even know where she was.

But somewhere in the back of her mind, while she lay unconscious, the girl heard the adults around her talking.

"She's going to be okay, Mrs Duran," said a voice.

"I just hope she wakes up," said her mother.

"How will the church manage without her?" asked a man's voice.

"I don't know," said another voice. "The youth centre really needs the help."

"I don't care about any of that," her mother said softly. "I just want her to open her eyes again."

The girl just lay there, unable to open her eyes, unable to move.

Deep in the back of her mind, the girl heard the voices.

They sound so sad, the girl thought. I wish I could help them.

Then she wished.

She wished hard.

BROTHERS

"Ow!" sixteen-year-old Forrest Summers shouted. "Nice one, Ben!"

Forrest and his younger brother, Ben, who was fourteen years old, were supposed to be carrying a big brown leather sofa into their new block of flats in River City.

They never made it to the first set of stairs.

Ben threw his hands up. "It wasn't my fault, Dad!"

"You dropped it on my foot!" Forrest yelled.

Mr Summers put down the heavy cardboard box he'd been carrying.

He walked between the brothers and asked, "Forrest, did you really think Benny would be able to carry that sofa with you? You should have waited for me."

"I can carry it!" Ben protested. "Forrest just twisted it wrong at the corner."

"That's enough," said Dad. "You take this box of dishes, Ben. Forrest, I'll help you with the sofa."

The boys and their father had been dragging things up the stairs all morning.

The climb to their new flat was five flights of stairs. Ben was sweating by the time he put the box of dishes in their new kitchen.

As he walked back down the stairs to get another box, he muttered to himself, "I wish we could have stayed in Montville."

His dad came down the steps behind him. "Now, Ben," Dad said, "we've been over this. My new job means we have to live here, in River City."

"Yeah," added Forrest, running down the stairs. "Stop whining. It's going to be more fun in the city anyway! Old Montville was boring-ville!"

Dad and Forrest passed Ben on the second floor landing and carried on down to the van. Ben lagged behind.

"I don't think it'll be more fun," Ben said to himself. "I already miss my friends from back home."

"Well, you'll make more friends," said a tiny voice from beside him.

Ben spun around.

Next to him was a girl about his age.

She had long black hair in a ponytail, and she was wearing shorts and a T-shirt that said "River City Youth Centre."

A skipping rope dangled from the girl's hand, and she was smiling at Ben.

"Hi," she said.

"Hi," Ben replied. He was blushing a little. He hoped she couldn't tell. "Do you live in the building?" he asked.

"No. Nearby," the girl said. "My name is Kaya."

"My name's Ben. We're moving in because my dad got a new job," Ben said.

"This is a nice building," Kaya replied. She headed down the stairs. "You'll like it. See you around, Ben!" she called.

Ben followed her downstairs to the main door.

But by the time he got outside, he only saw his father and brother unloading their rented van.

"Here you go, Benny," Forrest said, handing Ben another box to carry upstairs.

"Did you see a girl out here?" asked Ben.

"A girl?" Forrest asked, raising his eyebrows.

Ben ignored Forrest's eyebrows. "She came out of our building," Ben said. "She was holding a skipping rope. I was just talking to her on the stairs."

"Oh yeah?" said Forrest with a smile. "Hey, Dad! Ben has a girlfriend already!"

"Shut up!" Ben yelled.

Forrest laughed. "So, do you still miss Montville, Romeo?" he said with a chuckle. "You never had a girlfriend back home."

Forrest lightly punched his little brother in the shoulder.

"Okay, guys, that's enough," ordered Dad. "Let's get back to work."

Ben moved close to his brother and whispered, "She's not my girlfriend."

Then Ben quickly looked up and down the street. No sign of Kaya anywhere.

"Whoever she is," thought Ben, "She's pretty fast."

CHAPTER 2

THE GIRL IN THE ALLEY

That night for dinner, Dad brought home takeaway burgers and chips.

"I don't know about you boys, but after that hard work today, I'm starving," he said. He set down the bag of food on the kitchen table, and put a burger on each plate. "Chips are in the bag," he said. He grabbed his burger and took a big bite.

Forrest sighed with happiness. "I could eat ten of these."

"Me too," said Ben, taking a handful of chips and shoving them into his mouth.

"Benny's a big man, Dad," Forrest said. "He could eat ten burgers, and he's got himself a girlfriend."

Ben threw a chip at his brother's head.

"Forrest, stop picking on your brother," Dad said. He winked at Ben. "Just because he's already had more luck with the girls than you in the new neighbourhood is no reason to be jealous!"

Ben laughed, but Forrest didn't find it so funny. "Oh, ha ha, you two are a riot," Forrest said, getting up to grab a drink from the fridge.

"All right," Dad said after another chuckle. "Let's clean this up and get some sleep. It's been a long day, and we'll need to get up pretty early for church tomorrow."

* * *

That night, Ben collapsed onto his bed. He was worn out. His muscles ached. But he just couldn't get to sleep. He was too nervous about being in a new city. He'd have to make new friends and start at a new school in the autumn.

Ben had plenty of friends back home in Montville.

"Can't call it home anymore, though," he thought.

Ben had known those friends all his life. He didn't even remember meeting them. It was more like they were just always his friends.

"I'll never get to sleep," he said to himself, throwing off his blanket.

He got out of bed and walked over to the window. The view from his new window wasn't very nice. It was nothing like the view from his old room in Montville.

He closed his eyes and pictured the old tyre swing hanging from the big oak tree.

A creek lay beyond the tree, with an old wooden bridge crossing it. It was a very old bridge. Ben always thought it would fall apart whenever he stepped on it, but he loved it.

Ben wished he were back in Montville.

Maybe, if I wish hard enough, he thought.

He could almost smell the old lilac tree that grew next to his old bedroom window.

He could almost hear the whack of a bat as someone played baseball at the Montville Park. He could almost hear the neighbour's cat meowing in their back garden.

Now, Ben opened his eyes. Montville was a dream, far away in the night.

Instead, there was a dirty, old brick building next door. All the windows were dark.

Ben wondered if everyone in the city besides him was asleep.

Between Ben's block of flats and the dirty one next door was an alley.

Overflowing dustbins, torn bin liners, stray cats, and cardboard boxes littered the alley.

Suddenly, Ben heard a loud crash from below.

He looked down and saw that a dustbin had fallen over and hit the brick wall across the alley. At first he thought a cat must have jumped and knocked the can over.

After a few seconds, Ben could hear a person moving around in the alley below.

He leaned out the window and squinted down at the alley.

He couldn't see anyone.

A flickering streetlight shone into the alley, but it was still very dark.

Even so, staring past the railings of their fire escape, Ben could make out a girl playing in the alley.

It was Kaya, the girl he'd met on the stairs. The girl with the skipping rope.

"What is she doing out so late? And why's she playing in a dirty alley?" Ben asked himself.

He could hear laughing. He also heard the thumping of her feet each time they struck the hard ground.

Then he called down to the alley, "Hey! Kaya!"

The girl stopped jumping and looked up. Suddenly she wasn't smiling anymore. The streetlight still flickered, and made crooked shadows across her face.

She waved to him, and then turned and ran into the brick building next door.

"Wait!" Ben called, but the door slammed shut.

The girl was gone.

CHAPTER 3

SUNDAY MORNING

The next morning over breakfast, Dad turned to Ben and said, "Before your brother comes out of the shower, why don't you tell me about this girl you met yesterday."

Ben swallowed a bite of his eggs.

His father had always made the best scrambled eggs back in Montville. He added ham, cheese, onions, and peppers, and they'd always been his special Sunday morning breakfast.

Before church back in Montville, Dad would make those eggs for whoever came by.

Even though everyone was usually dressed in their best Sunday clothes, uncomfortable and itchy, the breakfast at the Summers house was always fun.

All of Ben's friends, his dad's friends and Forrest's friends, would sit in the big, crowded kitchen, eating Dad's eggs and laughing.

So Ben was relieved when he woke up that morning and smelled the familiar cooking. He was glad that he didn't have to leave those eggs behind in Montville.

"Well, her name is Kaya," Ben said.

He tried to picture her face in his mind, but besides her long ponytail and the T-shirt she wore, the image was fuzzy.

"She looks like she's my age, or maybe a year younger than me, I guess," he added.

Dad stood up and put his empty plate in the sink. "And she lives in the building?"

"I thought she did," replied Ben.

He remembered the door slamming shut the night before when Kaya had run into the building.

Slowly, he said, "But then I saw her playing in the alley last night, and then she ran into the building next door. So I think she lives there."

"Impossible!" called Forrest as he came into the room wearing just his bath towel. He was dripping wet.

Oh no, thought Ben. Forrest was eavesdropping!

Forrest grabbed a piece of toast. "That building is condemned," he said. "No one lives over there."

Forrest punched Ben in the shoulder and laughed. "It's worse than I thought! Benny has an imaginary girlfriend!"

"How do you know that building is condemned?" asked Ben.

"First of all," said Dad, "don't go walking around the house dripping all over the floor. Get dried off and dressed."

Dad sat back down at the table and sipped his coffee. "Second," he said, "just because a building has been condemned doesn't mean no one is living there."

"What do you mean?" said Ben.

"He means the homeless," said Forrest.

"I mean that not everyone is lucky enough to be able to live in a nice flat like ours," said Dad. "It's not rare for some families to set up a home wherever they can. Especially in a huge city like this one."

As his dad started doing the dishes and Forrest ran into his bedroom to get dressed, Ben glanced out the kitchen window.

Was Kaya homeless? Was that why she didn't tell him exactly where she lived?

CHAPTER 4

CHURCH LUNCH

Ben sat on the hard wooden pew, pulling at his collar and wondering why the church didn't have air conditioning. His bum was already asleep, and he was relieved when the preacher seemed to be wrapping things up.

The preacher smiled down at the people in the pews. He said, "Remember, everyone, we need your help more than ever since last week's robbery. Anything you can offer will go to replace the funds we'd already raised for the youth centre."

"That's a real shame," Dad whispered beside Ben. "Stealing from a preacher and a little girl."

Ben started to ask what he was talking about, but Dad shushed him.

That's grown-ups for you, thought Ben. It was all right for them to talk in church, but a kid wasn't allowed.

After the service, Ben, Forrest, and their dad walked out into the hallway.

Dad was busy introducing himself to the neighbours, and Forrest met a few kids his age who were hanging around before the church lunch.

Ben wandered down the hallway alone, looking at the pictures hanging along the walls.

He was homesick for Montville, and for all his old friends.

Something in one of the pictures caught his eye.

"Hmm," he thought, looking hard at the photo. "That girl looks like Kaya."

"What did you find, Benny?" Dad said as he joined Ben.

Ben pointed at the photo. "I think this is the girl I met yesterday on the stairs."

"Then I guess her family must go to our church," replied Dad. "Maybe you'll see her at the lunch."

Together they headed down to the basement.

The basement of the church was set up like a big canteen. There were about a dozen long folding tables. Each table had benches running along both sides. At one end of the room was another table, even longer than the others.

Several women, volunteers at the church who had brought the food for lunch, stood behind the longer table. They wore hairnets and aprons, and were spooning out mashed potatoes, vegetables, and chicken in breadcrumbs. A plate of cupcakes for dessert was at the far end of the table.

The food smelled so good. It seemed like hours before the Summer family reached the front of the queue. Ben didn't mind so much, since he was busy searching for Kaya in the dinner queue.

"Over here, boys," Dad said after they had got their plates of food. He had claimed three spots on a table in the middle of the room.

Ben kept his eyes open for Kaya. He could barely stay in his seat. After a few mouthfulls of food, he got up and walked around the big dining hall in the basement, just hoping to spot the girl.

"Benny!" called Forrest from the bench where he was still sitting with their father. "If you don't finish your chicken, I'm going to!"

Ben rolled his eyes. He went back to his seat and picked at his chicken.

"Miss your girlfriend?" said Forrest with a laugh.

Ben tried to ignore him. Instead he watched the other people at the lunch.

Everyone seemed to be having a good time, and a lot of people were dropping donations into the wooden box by the door.

One couple was sitting at the front table with the preacher. The man looked very upset, and the woman was crying.

The preacher seemed to be trying to comfort them.

"Who are they?" Ben asked, pointing.

Forrest shrugged and stole a piece of Ben's chicken.

"A lot of people turn to their preacher for comfort, Benny," his father reminded him. "Best to mind your own business, all right? Eat your lunch."

Ben nodded and ate a forkful of food.

But as he stared at the couple, he couldn't help feeling like he had seen them somewhere before.

CHAPTER 5

LAUGHTER

After the big lunch at church, Ben and his brother and father went home.

"You boys, get started on organizing your rooms," Dad said. "We've still got tonnes of boxes to unpack!"

Ben headed for his room. "One second, Benny," Dad said, stopping him in his tracks. "First, would you grab those two bags of rubbish from the kitchen and bring them down to the alley, where the dustbins are?"

"All right, Dad," Ben replied. He grabbed the stuffed bags from the kitchen and started down the stairs.

* * *

The alley was even more disgusting during the day. Ben could clearly see all the litter and smell all the horrible rubbish.

Lots of bags were just lying on the street in the alley, rather than being inside a dustbin like they should have been.

Most of those bags were torn – probably by rats, Ben thought – and their stinky contents spilled out all over the pavement.

Ben dropped the bags into a bin near the back of the alley, and then walked back towards the front of the building.

He stopped for a moment in front of a door – the one he saw Kaya use the night before.

He grabbed the door handle, trying to decide if he should open it.

A chill ran up and down his back.

It was a weird feeling. It was the same feeling he had once on Halloween back in Montville, when he had dared to trick-or-treat at the old Tyler Mansion, which everyone said was haunted.

He had scared himself silly that night. He had been thinking and worrying so much about seeing a ghost that he actually saw one. Or thought that he did.

"This is ridiculous," Ben muttered to himself. "It's just an old building!"

The door handle felt cold. "Of course it's cold," thought Ben. "It's metal."

Then the handle turned colder. As if it was turning into ice.

Ben pulled his hand away.

"Benny!" It was his dad's voice. Ben looked up and saw his father leaning out the window. "Come on up and get to work on your room!" his dad called down.

Ben stood for a moment in front of the door, trying to feel annoyed at his dad.

But for some reason, he was almost relieved to go back upstairs.

* * *

Ben sighed when he stepped into his bedroom. Most of his bags and boxes were still packed up, and his walls were completely bare.

"This will take all afternoon!" he thought.

Ben emptied a suitcase onto his bed. All his clothes and the extra sheets and blankets for his bed came tumbling out.

"Ugh," he said, looking down at the pile he'd have to fold and put away.

The big meal at church had made him tired. He flopped on to the bed.

"Maybe I can just lie down for a little while," he thought.

A little while turned into several hours.

When Ben next opened his eyes, the Sun was already going down. He stretched and yawned, then went into the living room.

Dad was there, dozing on the couch. His brother's door was closed, and Ben thought the lunch must have made all three of them very tired.

"I guess everyone's taking a nap," he muttered to himself.

Then he heard happy laughter coming from his room.

Kaya?

He ran into his room and looked out the open window. He was just in time to see the girl down below dart into the building next door.

"Not this time," he said. He slipped on his trainers, grabbed his torch, and ran out of the flat.

CHAPTER 6

THE ALLEY

With the Sun so low, the alley was already growing dim.

The light from the flickering streetlamp made everything look as if it were moving.

Dustbins seemed to creep along the ground.

A fire escape appeared to shudder and shiver against the brick wall.

Ben jumped when a rat came running from behind a cardboard box.

"What am I so scared of?" he asked

himself, laughing. "It's just the alley! I was here a few hours ago, and nothing happened."

Ben forced himself to laugh again. "There's nothing scary about this place. Gross, yes. But, scary? No."

He quickly found the door he'd seen Kaya run into. This time, he didn't wait.

He just grabbed the door and yanked it open. It was very heavy, and it creaked a little, but it did open.

Silently, Ben stuck his head into the doorway and looked inside.

He clicked on his torch and shone it into a long corridor.

His torch shed light on some rubbish on the floor, cracked tiles, and peeling paint on the ceiling and the walls. The plaster was mouldy and crumbling away in some places.

"Forrest was right," Ben whispered to himself. "This building is abandoned. No one could live here."

Suddenly Ben felt something scurry across his foot and he jumped.

"It's just a rat," he said to himself, looking down. The dirty rodent squealed and darted through the open door and out into the alley.

"Relax, Summers," Ben told himself.

Pulling the door open further, Ben stepped inside. "Hello?" he said.

He heard laughter, but it wasn't Kaya's happy laughter.

This laughter came from a man, and it wasn't happy. It sounded to Ben like mocking and mean laughter. Chills ran up and down his back again.

"This is a bad idea," Ben thought.

He thought of turning back, but then he stopped. What if Kaya was in trouble?

He tiptoed through the dark corridor until he came to an open door. A light was shining inside.

Ben peeked around the door and saw two older boys sitting on boxes.

They had their backs to the door, and in front of them was a big metal bin with a fire burning in it.

Ben thought the boys looked a little older than his brother.

One had spiky red hair. The other had a smooth, shaved head.

The boys were looking at a newspaper and laughing and talking loudly.

The redheaded boy kept pointing at the newspaper and reading out loud.

Then both boys would laugh and mutter things to each other.

"I don't like the look of this," Ben thought.

He wondered what Kaya was doing coming into a place like this.

He decided to head home. Something about this place seriously creeped him out. And the boys there were clearly up to no good.

Ben started to turn around, but as he did, he put his foot down on another scurrying rat.

The creature squealed and jumped.

"What was that?" asked the guy with the shaved head.

Ben froze.

The boy stood up from the box and turned to the door.

"Uh-oh," Ben thought. "I better get out of here!"

"Hey!" called the spiky redhead. "Hey you!" Ben could hear anger in the boy's voice.

"Stop that kid!" one of them yelled.

Both older boys started for the door – and for Ben.

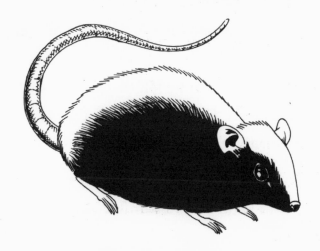

CHAPTER 7

CHASE

Ben ran as fast as he could back towards the door to the alley. He heard the older boys' boots stomping on the tiled floor behind him.

Ben's heart pounded in his chest and his feet pounded down on the cracked tile floor. He ran so fast that he felt the blood beating in his throat. "Hey, you little brat!" one of the boys yelled.

Ben nearly tripped when he turned the corner to head back towards the alley.

His old trainers barely gripped the worn tile, and his right foot went out from under him. His shoulder banged into the crumbling plaster wall. Somehow he managed to stay on his feet, but the boys were getting closer.

"Stop!" one of them yelled.

Ben didn't stop. He ran as hard as he could, right into the heavy door, and the door swung open.

The smells of the night air and the stench of the building's trash struck his nostrils just as he stumbled out into the alley.

The boys were close behind him, so Ben pushed a dustbin over as he ran out of the alley. He heard it fall, and then heard the older boys banging into it.

They yelled, and swore at him, but Ben had escaped.

* * *

"Where have you been?" Forrest said when Ben came into the apartment, panting and sweaty.

"Um, nowhere," Ben said. "I just went for a walk."

"Why are you so sweaty?" Forrest asked, raising his eyebrows.

"Why are you up?" asked Ben, trying to change the subject.

"I was hungry," said Forrest, "and I heard some banging outside in the alley. So answer my question."

"Uh, I met some kids and played some basketball," Ben said.

Ben didn't like to lie to Forrest. He knew his brother might be able to protect him from the two older boys, but he also knew that Forrest would make fun of him for going into the old building to look for his "new girlfriend."

Besides, what chance would Forrest and Ben have against those two boys?

The boys looked like they'd been in a lot of fights before. They looked like they usually won those fights, too.

* * *

That evening, when he climbed into bed, Ben wasn't tired at all.

He tossed and turned for a while.

His mind kept going back to Kaya, the old building next door, and those tough older boys.

Finally, Ben threw off his blanket and went to the window.

It was late, after eleven o'clock.

Ben doubted Kaya would be down in the alley, but as he went to the window, he heard her cheery laughter.

He heard the thumping of her feet as she skipped.

The girl saw Ben right away, and she stopped smiling.

She waved to him, and Ben thought she wanted him to come down and follow her into the old building.

"Do you need help?" asked Ben. "Should I follow you?"

Kaya nodded to him, then she turned and disappeared through the door.

I have to follow her! Ben said to himself. I have to know what she's doing in that old building. She can't be friends with those guys. They must be trying to hurt her!

Ben threw on a pair of jeans and a T-shirt and started for his bedroom door, but as he opened it, he noticed the light was still on in the living room.

"Dad is still awake," he thought. "I can't sneak out with him in the living room!"

Then he heard voices. Who can be visiting at this hour? Ben wondered.

Leaving his bedroom door open a crack, Ben took a few steps down the hall. He leaned forward, straining to hear what his father was saying.

"It's such a shame," Dad said.

"Indeed," said the other man's voice. "Without that money, we won't be able to maintain the youth centre for much longer."

Ben realized it was the preacher from church.

"And that poor girl!" Dad added.

"Mrs Duran is very upset, of course, " the preacher replied. "The doctors think her daughter will be okay, but for now, she still won't wake up."

"Well, we'll be thinking of her and her family," Dad said. "Maybe I'll have Benny go over to the centre tomorrow. I'll be at work, and I'd like my older boy to go out looking for some summer work."

"We'd enjoy having him," the preacher replied. It sounded like he was heading out the door. "There are lots of great kids down there every day this summer."

Suddenly Ben felt a tickle in his nose.

Oh, not now, he thought. He grabbed his nose and stopped the sneeze. But as he stepped backwards, the floor beneath him gave a loud squeak.

"Benny? Forrest? Is that you?" his dad called from the door. "Darn," Ben thought. He dived back into bed."

"Sorry, Kaya," he whispered to himself. "I don't think I can escape tonight."

CHAPTER 8

THE YOUTH CENTRE

"So you wait here until I come and pick you up, okay, Ben?" Forrest said when the two of them reached the front door to the youth centre the next morning.

The River City Youth Centre was a big brick building attached to the back of the church.

A few kids around Ben's age were hanging around at the front.

Ben could hear yelling and laughter coming from inside.

"I'll be fine," Ben told his brother. "Good luck with the job search."

Forrest rolled his eyes. "Like I want a job," he said as he walked off.

Ben thought his brother looked miserable in his Sunday clothes on a hot Monday morning.

"Hello, Ben," said the preacher as Ben walked into the youth centre. "Your father said you'd be coming along today."

"Hi," Ben replied, taking in the scene.

There were three ping-pong tables at the back, and a small basketball court where a bunch of boys were playing.

In the nearest corner, some younger kids were playing board games. A few even littler kids were running around, screaming and laughing.

"Feel free to look around, or join in any of the games," the preacher said. Then he walked away.

Ben watched him walk through the door that connected the youth centre to the church. Ben wondered if there would be any adults at the centre at all. It seemed like the whole room was full of kids.

Then he spotted a woman helping a small boy play with some blocks. She looked familiar. After he thought about it for a few seconds, he realized that she was the woman who the preacher had comforted during the church lunch.

"Who are you?" said a voice next to Ben.

Ben turned and saw a boy standing beside him holding a ping-pong paddle.

"What?" Ben asked. He'd heard the boy's question, but he felt confused.

"I said, who are you?" the boy said. "I saw you at church yesterday. You were walking around like you'd lost something. Are you new here or something?"

"Yeah," Ben replied. "We just moved here a couple of days ago."

"A couple of days? Wow! You are new," the boy said. "I'm Will."

"My name's Ben," Ben replied. "Hey, who is that woman over there?" He nodded towards the woman with the little boy.

"That's Mrs Duran," Will explained. "She volunteers here sometimes. She's really nice."

"I saw her at the church lunch," Ben said. "Um, I think she was crying," he added in a soft whisper.

Will squinted in thought, and then nodded. "Oh, right. Her daughter is in the hospital," he explained.

"Really? What happened to her?" Ben asked.

Will shrugged. "She was hurt by a couple of thugs. We call them the Preacher Bandits, because they stole the youth centre money from the preacher."

"They stole from the preacher?" asked Ben. "That's pretty awful."

"He was walking Mrs Duran's daughter home from the youth centre when they were attacked," Will explained.

"Wow," Ben said. "Did the police catch the bandits?"

"Nope," Will replied. "The preacher blacked out, and when he woke up, the thugs were gone. And so was all the money that had been donated for the youth centre."

Will paused, looking around. Then he leaned in close to Ben.

Will said, "The preacher says if we don't get more money soon, he may have to shut down the youth centre for good."

"That's awful!" Ben said.

Will nodded. "Yup. And Mrs Duran's daughter was unconscious."

He leaned closer to Ben and looked around, before adding in a whisper, "Some people are saying she'll never wake up."

CHAPTER 9

NOT DREAMING

Ben stayed at the youth centre almost all day, playing ping-pong and basketball with Will and some other boys he met.

Ben was beginning to think living in River City wouldn't be too bad after all.

When Forrest came to pick him up, Ben didn't want to leave yet.

"Come on, Mr Popular," Forrest joked. "Dad'll worry if we're not home when he gets back."

"See you tomorrow," Will told Ben.

That night, Ben lay in bed, trying to come up with ways to save the youth centre.

Maybe a car wash, or a bake sale, to make money, he thought, while he drifted off to sleep.

As he was nodding off, he heard a small voice.

Someone was calling his name.

"That's impossible," Ben thought. He closed his eyes tight.

"Ben . . ."

It was a gentle voice. It seemed to float into his bedroom on the breeze that brushed his shoulder. Ben shivered.

"Ben . . . ," the voice said again.

"I know I'm not dreaming," Ben said to himself.

He got out of bed and opened his door.

In the living room, Dad was sitting on the couch and watching TV.

"Did you call me?" Ben asked.

"No, I didn't," Dad replied. "You must have been dreaming."

"Oh," Ben replied. "That makes sense." But he knew he hadn't been asleep.

"Get back to bed. It's late," Dad said.

Ben closed his door and sat on the edge of his bed.

"It must have been Kaya," Ben thought. "And I think something very weird is going on. This time, I'm going down to the alley as soon as Dad is asleep. Kaya needs help!"

* * *

Ben was asleep before he knew it.

"Ben . . ."

He woke up with a start and sat up on the edge of his bed. "Oh no!" Ben said out loud. "I must have fallen asleep." He glanced at the clock.

"One a.m.?" he thought. "I've been asleep for hours! I wonder if Kaya is still waiting for me."

"Ben . . ."

It was the same gentle voice, as though Kaya had heard his thought and wanted to let him know that she was indeed waiting.

The breeze coming through Ben's open window gave him a chill, even though it was a hot night.

Quietly, Ben got to his feet and got dressed in jeans and a T-shirt, which were lying on his bedroom floor. He slowly opened his bedroom door.

The apartment was almost completely silent.

He was glad to see that the lights and the TV were off.

The only noise he could hear was his dad snoring in his room.

The coast was clear.

Minutes later, Ben was gripping his torch and slowly walking into the alley.

This time, he wasn't afraid of the little noises he heard. He was too busy worrying about the tough older boys he'd escaped from the night before.

Once again, he pulled open the heavy door that led into the old brick building.

"Kaya?" he whispered.

Ben shone the torch in all directions, but the corridor was empty.

He crept up to where the corridor ended in a 'T' shape. He shone his light in both directions.

The whole first floor looked deserted.

"Kaya?" he said. "Are you here?"

"Ben . . ." The voice was as soft as a breeze.

Ben heard some rustling coming from around the corner at the end of the hall.

He pointed his flashlight in the direction of the noise and voice.

A pale face stared back at him.

It was Kaya.

Ben almost yelled in surprise. There hadn't been anyone in the hallway a second ago. He was sure of it. He had been alone.

Kaya came from nowhere!

He squinted down the hall. Kaya was standing there, but not completely.

It was like she was only partly standing there.

Partly there?

Ben didn't understand it.

Kaya was standing there, but the beam from Ben's torch seemed to shine right through her. It lit up the wall behind where the girl was standing.

"That's impossible," he thought.

The girl giggled.

Then she darted around a corner, out of sight.

"Kaya?" Ben ran to the corner, calling after her. "Kaya, where are you?"

Suddenly, a strong hand grabbed his shoulder.

The grip was so strong that it almost hurt.

The hand spun Ben around and he found himself face to face with the boys who had chased him the night before.

The taller one leant over and gritted his teeth in Ben's face. "You shouldn't have come back here, punk!"

THERE'S NO GIRL HERE

"What should we do with him?" the red-haired boy said.

Ben sat on a box, feeling small and weak, while the two tough boys walked in circles around him. They punched their open hands like they were going to beat him up. They had tied him up with rope and tape, and the pressure hurt his wrists and arms.

"I don't know," answered the other guy. "Maybe we should put him in the hospital, like we did with that girl!"

Both boys laughed.

Ben was more angry than frightened. He was angry that they might hurt Kaya, just like they had attacked that other girl, the Duran's daughter, and the preacher.

He was too angry to hold his tongue.

"Which girl are you talking about?" Ben asked. "Are you talking about the girl that came running into this building?" Both older boys stopped laughing.

"There's no girl in this building," said the redhead.

"The little girl with the skipping rope," Ben replied. "She comes running in here every night. I was looking for her. That's why I came in."

Both older boys looked surprised. Ben thought they even seemed a little worried.

"Take his torch and go and check it out," the boy with the shaved head said to his friend.

He frowned at Ben before continuing, "I'll stay here and keep an eye on our 'guest.'"

"All right," said the other boy.

He picked up Ben's torch, which had fallen on the ground when they'd grabbed Ben, and started searching the corridors.

Ben heard laughter, Kaya's happy laughter, coming from the one of the corridors.

"This better not be a joke, brat," said the guy with the shaved head. He sat down on a box across from Ben and stared at him.

"Can't you hear her?" Ben said. "She's laughing."

"Shh!" the older boy said. He strained to listen.

Ben heard the laughter again.

Then, in the dim light, he saw the little girl run past the open door of the room.

"I don't hear anything," the older boy finally said.

"But she's laughing, and running through the corridors," Ben insisted. "Didn't you see her run by just now?"

The older boy stared at Ben. "I don't know what your game is, kid," he said, "but I don't find it funny, you know what I mean?" He waved his fist at Ben. "Now knock it off!"

Again Ben heard Kaya's happy laughter.

It rang through the whole building like a windchime through the rolling hills back in Montville.

Ben couldn't understand why his captor didn't hear it, but he kept his mouth shut.

"No use making the guys angrier than they already are," he thought.

"There's no one else here, Jay," a voice said.

The redheaded boy was back and standing in the doorway.

"This kid's messing with us," the redhead added. He looked at Ben threateningly and crossed his arms across his chest.

"That's what I thought," said Jay. "And now he's going to get it."

Both older boys started walking towards Ben, fists clenched, ready to attack.

Laughter echoed just outside the doorway.

"It's her," said Ben. "Right there. Right outside the door. Kaya, look out!" he yelled.

"What are you trying to pull, kid?" the guy demanded. He crept closer to Ben.

Ben felt his captors' breath on his face as he struggled with the tape and rope on his wrists.

"You think we're dumb enough to fall for that old trick?" the redhead said. "Ha! There's no one else here."

"That's what you think!" someone shouted, and both older boys were grabbed from behind.

11

CHAPTER

SAVED!

The older boys turned to throw punches.

Jay was able to defend himself for a
moment, but the redheaded boy fell to
the ground.

Ben squinted in the dim light to see who
was saving him.

He was able to make out two police
officers, because of their hats.

Someone else was standing behind them,
but Ben couldn't tell who it was.

It was hard to see past the fighting figures in front of him, but then the other shadow stepped further into the room.

"Forrest!" Ben called out.

His older brother squeezed past the struggling police and thugs.

"It's a good thing you're such a rubbish sneak," Forrest said, untying his brother. "I heard you close the door to the flat and followed you."

Forrest sat on a box next to Ben.

The brothers watched as the two police officers handcuffed Jay and his partner and led them out of the room.

"I saw you creep into the alley and then pull open that old door," Forrest continued. "What in the world did you think you were doing over here?"

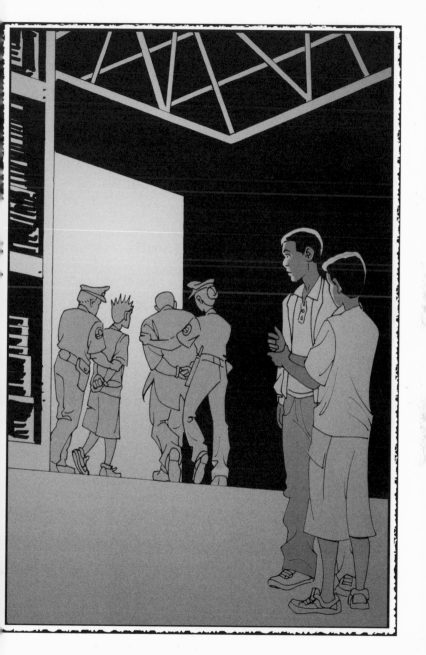

"Where'd the police come from?" Ben asked. "How did you know I was in trouble?"

Forrest wrinkled his forehead. "What? I didn't know!"

"What do you mean?" asked Ben. "Didn't you come in with the police?"

"Well," Forrest replied. He looked at his hands and frowned before continuing. "That's the weird thing. I was about to follow you inside. I just wanted to scare you a little, maybe pretend I was going to squeal on you to Dad, since you shouldn't have been sneaking out in the middle of the night in the first place."

Forrest paused. He glanced around the room with a confused look on his face.

"But then," he continued, "then I heard someone calling me."

"Calling you?" Ben asked.

"Yes," his brother replied. "From somewhere outside the alley. Just this little tiny voice, saying, 'Forrest . . . Forrest . . .'"

Ben got a chill.

It must have been Kaya!

"For a second I thought it was you," Forrest said. "I thought maybe you were fooling around. I thought that you'd come out another door of the building and were playing a joke on me, like I'd been planning to play on you. So I ran around to the front."

"And?" Ben prompted.

"And there was no one there. At least no one calling my name," Forrest said.

"There were these two police officers, though," he added. "I told them you were inside the building and they decided they'd better come and get you. The building's condemned, so it's not safe to be in."

"So who was calling you?" Ben said.

Forrest shrugged. "I don't know, but it was very lucky I found the police before coming in after you."

Ben knew it wasn't luck.

It was Kaya.

CHAPTER 12

HEROES

"Well, it looks like you boys are heroes," said one of the police officers.

"Heroes?" Forrest said, getting up from the box he was sitting on.

"What do you mean?" asked Ben, also getting to his feet. "All I did was get into some trouble, then get rescued!"

Ben thought the police and Forrest had been the heroes.

The police officer laughed.

"You boys just found the two thieves who attacked the preacher," said the other officer.

He held up a wooden box. "This is the youth centre fund!"

Forrest's jaw dropped. "I can't believe I was face to face with the Preacher Bandits!" he said, stunned.

Forrest's eyes lit up. "One of them actually punched me!" he cried out.

He stroked his jaw and smiled.

Ben wrinkled his forehead. "And I can't believe Kaya led me here."

"Where was Kaya?" he wondered.

* * *

The rest of the night was a blur.

Dad had turned up soon after the arrests were made. He was worried.

Then the police had to take Ben's and Forrest's statements about everything that had happened.

Ben tried to explain that a little girl had come into the building ahead of him.

"You guys have to go look for her," he told the police officers. "She's probably still in the building somewhere."

But the policemen shook their heads.

"She must have got out some other way," one of them said.

"That's right," said the other police officer. "Our officers did a very thorough search of the entire building. They didn't find anyone else at all."

"That's really weird," Ben said.

"Sorry, kid," the officer said. "I don't know what to tell you."

It was almost sunrise by the time the Summers men made it back to their apartment.

Dad wasn't happy to have to rush off to work after getting no sleep. "I could really use a nap," he said. He shook his head and walked into his bedroom as Forrest and Ben flopped down on the living room sofa.

Dad reappeared a few minutes later, dressed in his work clothes. Then he stood over the sink to eat a quick bowl of cereal.

"Forrest, you get out there and look for some work again, all right?" he asked as he left the apartment.

"Okay, Dad," Forrest replied as the door closed.

Then he turned to Ben.

"I'll take you to the youth centre again," Forrest said. "Sound good?"

"Okay," Ben replied.

"We'll probably be welcomed like heroes!" Forrest said with a laugh.

After eating a quick breakfast, the brothers left the flat. They were tired, but they had a strange kind of energy from their exciting night.

At the youth centre, they were indeed welcomed like heroes.

Everyone cheered as they walked in.

A big banner hung from the ceiling, saying "Thanks from River City Youth Centre." A big chocolate cake sat waiting for them on a table in the middle of the room.

Some icing spelled out "Hooray for the Summers boys!"

"Well done, Ben!" said Will, patting Ben on the back.

"Atta boy, Ben," said the preacher.

Mrs Duran gave Ben a big hug. "Thank you, Ben!" she said. She had tears in her eyes, but she was smiling.

"Can I challenge the hero to a rematch of ping-pong?" Will asked, holding out two paddles.

"Sure!" Ben said. For the first time, he realized that Will was becoming his first real friend in his new city.

Ben grabbed a paddle from him, and the two boys started for the tables. But Mrs Duran and the preacher stopped them.

"Before you do that, Ben," said Mrs Duran, "I know someone else who'd like to meet you." Her smile grew even bigger.

"Yes," said the preacher. "Mrs Duran's daughter has woken up, and she'd like to meet the boys who helped catch her attackers!"

13

CHAPTER

THE HOSPITAL

Mrs Duran, the preacher, Ben, and Forrest walked to the hospital together.

"Don't you have to go look for a job?" Ben asked his brother as they walked down the city sidewalks.

Forrest shrugged. "Of course, but I can take an hour or so first. I really want to meet the little girl," he replied. "Besides, Dad wouldn't mind a little detour for his sons, the heroes!"

The brothers laughed.

Then they stopped in front of a large brick building. "This is it," Mrs Duran said. The automatic hospital doors slid open, and the four of them walked in silence down the long white corridors.

The tiles clicked and clacked under Mrs Duran's shoes as they walked. Ben smelled bleach and cleaning fluid and flowers.

"This way," the preacher said, and the four of them stepped into a large lift.

A man on a trolley was also in the elevator, along with two nurses in funny outfits. One of the nurses had little pictures of cats on her clothes, and the other had lollipops and other kinds of sweets on her clothes.

Mrs Duran pressed the button for the fourth floor. The bell dinged three times, and then they all stepped out of the lift.

A sign on the wall said "Children's Ward."

Ben and Forrest quietly followed Mrs Duran and the preacher down the corridor.

Finally they came to a door marked "424," and Mrs Duran hurried in. The preacher followed. Ben and Forrest exchanged a look, then they went in too.

Mrs Duran was talking to someone in a bed behind a curtain.

"Kaya, dear," said Mrs Duran. "Here are Ben and Forrest Summers."

"Kaya?" thought Ben. He stepped further into the room and peeked around the curtain.

"Kaya!" he cried. It was the girl from the alley! But what was she doing lying in this hospital bed?

Forrest stepped past the curtain. "That's impossible, Ben," he whispered to his brother.

"Thank you," Kaya said to the brothers. "I knew it had to work."

The preacher and Mrs Duran looked confused. "What had to work, sweetheart?" Mrs Duran asked.

"Do you kids know each other already?" the preacher asked. He looked from Kaya to Ben and back.

Kaya smiled. "Not exactly," she said. "Let's just say I met Ben and Forrest in a dream I was having."

"A dream?" asked Mrs Duran.

"Something like that," Ben said.

Kaya laughed. Ben knew the laugh as well as he knew the summer breezes back in Montville.

"River City won't be so bad after all," he thought, smiling.

RIVER CITY

Life in River City did turn out to be pretty good for Ben Summers.

He spent a lot of time at the newly renovated River City Youth Centre, and his two new best friends, Will and Kaya, were always with him.

One afternoon, Ben and Kaya were playing ping-pong. Kaya had beaten Ben for the third game straight, and he decided he needed a break.

"Ha," said Kaya. "Can't take any more, huh?"

Ben shook his head.

The two sat down to watch Will playing basketball.

"I still don't get it, Kaya," said Ben. "I mean, I know that somehow you helped me to find the youth centre's donations. But how?"

"I know," replied Kaya. She took his hand. "I don't really get it either."

"There's no such thing as ghosts, right?" said Ben.

He glanced down at his hands and blushed a little. "And besides, you weren't, I mean, you were just asleep, right?"

"Right. I wasn't dead," said Kaya, "if that's what you mean."

Her face turned sad for a moment.

"But I was trapped inside my own head, and all I had to do all day was wish and dream," she said quietly.

Ben knew how powerful dreams could be. He remembered how he had stood at the window of his new bedroom that first night in the city. And he remembered how he had thought about Montville.

"So, you dreamt about me?" asked Ben.

Kaya nodded. "Yes. I don't know why, though. All I know is that I wished that somehow, by the time I woke up, the youth centre would be saved."

Ben sighed, and both of them were silent for a minute.

Finally, Ben took a deep breath and said, "Well, how about a rematch, then?"

He got up and grabbed a paddle and the ping-pong ball, and bounced it on the table.

"Sure," said Kaya, hopping up and grabbing her own paddle. "You might win. After all, if you wish for something hard enough, anything can happen!"

Ben rolled his eyes, but he knew she was right.

ABOUT THE AUTHOR

Steve Brezenoff lives with his wife, Beth, and their small, smelly dog, Harry. Besides writing books, he enjoys playing computer games, riding his bicycle, and helping secondary school students to improve their own writing skills. Steve's ideas almost always come to him in dreams, so he does his best writing in his pyjamas.

ABOUT THE ILLUSTRATOR

Cynthia Martin has worked in comics and animation since 1983. Her credits include *Star Wars, Spiderman,* and *Wonder Woman* for Marvel Comics and DC Comics, in addition to work as a storyboard artist for Sony Children's Entertainment and the Krislin Company. Cynthia's recent projects include an extensive series of graphic novels for Capstone Press and two issues of *Blue Beetle* for DC Comics.

GLOSSARY

abandoned left alone and empty

alley narrow passageway between or behind buildings

bandits robbers, usually a group

captor someone who catches another person

condemned unsafe to live in

deserted empty, abandoned

imaginary something that exists in the imagination but not the real world

maintain keep in good condition

pew long bench that people sit on in church

preacher head of a church

straining trying very hard

unconscious not awake, not able to see, feel, or think

1. Has your family ever had to move? How did you feel? What did you like about your new place, and what did you miss about your old home? If you haven't moved, how have you felt when someone new moved to your town, school, or neighbourhood? Talk about it.

2. Forrest teases Ben by saying that Kaya is his girlfriend. How would you respond if someone teased you like that?

3. Do you believe in things like out-of-body experiences? Why or why not?

1. The Youth Centre becomes an important part of Ben and Forrest's lives. Do you have a place like that? Where is it? Who have you met there? Write about it.

2. In this book, Kaya dreams about meeting Ben. What else happens in her dream? Who else does she dream about? Write a page that describes another part of Kaya's dream.

3. Ben and Forrest's old home was in a smaller town, but they move to a large city. Would you rather live in a small town or a big city? Explain your answers.

WHAT HAPPENED

A coma is a condition in which a person cannot wake up, often as a result of a serious injury. Of course, when a person is in a coma, she cannot speak and cannot make her thoughts known to her friends and family.

Then how did Kaya meet Ben on the stairs of his new block of flats? How did she call to him from the alley in the middle of the night?

Well, this was just a story, of course. But for thousands of years, many different societies believed that some people could actually leave their bodies and enter a spirit realm. This is often called "astral travel," but you might have heard the term "out of body experience."

In ancient China, for example, people known as shamans claimed to enter the spirit world to affect the weather or to help a sick person.

Among some Native American tribes, people leave their bodies in search of the solution to difficult problems in their lives, often following special spirit guides through the weird and scary spirit realm.

Some people from all walks of life believe they have left their bodies during a very vivid dream. Often they have dreamt of a loved one who has passed away. When they wake up, they are certain they have had a nice visit with that person.

So who's to say if Kaya would be able to contact Ben? She might have been so angry and so in need of help that she was able to do something magical. After all, Kaya wanted those Preacher Bandits caught!

The Curse of the Wendigo
by Scott R. Welvaert

Agate and Buck set out on a spine-tingling adventure through the haunted Canadian woods in search of their missing parents. An ancient curse is set into motion, and soon they too are being hunted.

Rock Art Rebel
by M. J. Cosson

Beto's urban art is labelled graffiti by the police, so the boy is sent to spend the summer with relatives. Then Beto discovers art in an unexpected place, and he's the only one who can save it.

The Ghost's Revenge
by M. Peschke

The ancient Comanche warrior that Zack sees in his dreams has begun to appear in real life. As the line between real life and Zack's dream world blurs, he embarks on a dangerous journey of terror and discovery.

Poison Plate
by M. Sobel Spirn

When Mark moves in with a family who owns a restaurant, he is wrongfully accused of whipping up a diabolically delicious dinner.